MINDSCAPES

POEMS FOR THE REAL WORLD

OTHER COLLECTIONS BY RICHARD PECK

SOUNDS AND SILENCES

POETRY FOR NOW

EDGE OF AWARENESS

25 CONTEMPORARY ESSAYS

(Ned E. Hoopes, co-editor)

DELACORTE PRESS, NEW YORK

MINDSCAPES
POEMS FOR THE REAL WORLD
EDITED BY RICHARD PECK
66084
I.C.C. LIBRARY

Library of Congress Catalog Card Number: 70-146821
Manufactured in the United States of America
Second Printing—1974

FOR JEAN ANN
AND RICHARD HUGHES,
KRISTIN
AND COURTNEY

TABLE OF CONTENTS

THE STRONG MEN KEEP COMING ON

THE ROAD ALL RUNNERS COME

I'LL MAKE ME A WORLD

WHAT DO I *REALLY* LOOK LIKE?

LET ME CELEBRATE YOU

INTRODUCTION

Poetry explores the landscapes of the mind, and it expands the mind, moving both writer and reader out into wider fields, all ripe for further discovery. But poetry isn't entirely an experience of the mind, for today's poetry confronts the actual and the external, stressing the real over the ideal, the compassionate over the sentimental. It provides new ways of looking at a world observable to us all.

Some poets have kept diaries, but they don't confuse their diaries with their poems. A poem tends to look out, not in, even when it explores the poet's deepest, most private, most lonely self. It looks out in two ways: First the poet translates the personal into a form —maybe a very original one, but a form nonetheless. Then he looks beyond the form to the reader—to the people he may never meet anywhere but through his poem.

Once the poet has decided to share it, has crafted it, honed it until every word counts, then it truly finds another landscape, for it takes on a new meaning with every reader. Unlike the diary that is meant for only one pair of eyes, the poem develops a new life each time a reader brings his experience to it.

When does the poet decide to share? Usually in a moment when he is at his most intense—a moment when something perhaps overwhelming has struck him, though it may be something almost unnoticeable to others around him. There was a time when poets were thought to be divinely inspired; today, their inspiration appears more earth-bound. There was a time when love suggested exaggerated praise of the beloved. Today it's liable to translate:

> I'd rather
> heave half a brick than say
> I love you, though I do

The old, time-honored themes of love, death, and nature deserve these new interpretations, even if they jar. Joining the traditional inspirations are the new stimuli of our mechanized, urbanized, transistorized century. The world we know now surely has more than its share of intense moments, fertile fields for a poet's perspective.

Many people have been permanently turned off poetry early in their lives. Often, the form of the poem stood more as a barrier between poet and reader than as a connection. Older poetry seemed to lurk behind literary terms that required memorizing, words like *sonnet, metaphor,* and *iambic pentameter,* for a start. Modern poetry, with its new look on the page and its rejection of the old conventions, often seems to deal exclusively in masks and mysteries, full of word traps and pattern mazes requiring deep analysis and specialized training. But these are the concerns of people who think poetry is chiefly an exercise rather than a shared communication. *Mindscapes* is designed to emphasize communication through a collection of poems, mostly modern, that deal in encounters with a real, hectic, unpretty, and recognizable world.

The motorcyclist, who is also a poet, sees the open road ahead of him, of his machine, of us as a "blacksnake across the furrows of America." The observer of a sports car flipped over and burning in a wheat field sees with a mechanic's eye "German steel built like a water-drop." A sky-diver whose chute fails to open falls "without a sound, like a rock in a handkerchief." The life of a burned-out basketball star is captured in a single, stark line:

"He never learned a trade, he just sells gas."

Suddenly we're there—wherever the poet wants us to be—with him and sharing. A great deal is said these days in very few words. We are usually given the image and left to flesh it out with our own experience. This condensation of idea makes for maximum impact. All the uncertainty of a young girl, alone in her room before the mirror, speaks simply in:

"What do I *really* look like?"

And all the newspaper and television coverage of a moonshot is distilled in eight ordinary words:

The rocket tore a tunnel through the sky

Poetry, then, can offer the manageable message, brief enough to read and talk over together with others; unexpected in its range of subjects—high school bands, lynchings, business machines, science fiction; and cosmic in its perceptions—of tyrants and astronauts, cowboys and Bowery bums, movie monsters and boxers, a full spectrum of experience shrewdly and humanly observed.

Mindscapes is a collection of poems for everyone, whatever his goals and interests. It's meant, simply, to draw readers and poets together on the common ground we all inhabit, and to lead us on together into some of the many worlds around us, familiar and uncharted.

RICHARD PECK
Washington, D.C.

GOOD TIMES AND MONEY

PLAN

My cousin Max is being married
on a quiz show.
He is getting a Westinghouse refrigerator
a Singer sewing machine
a set of furniture from Sears and Roebuck
an ant farm
a General Electric toaster
and a girl.

It is not enough.
He expects babies and happiness
good times and money
and a government that wars on war.

My cousin Max expects too much.

ROD MCKUEN

REEL ONE

It was all technicolor
from bullets to nurses.
The guns gleamed like cars
and blood was as red
as the paint on dancers.
The screen shook with fire
and my bones whistled.
It was like life, but better.

I held my girl's hand,
in the deepest parts,
and we walked home, after,
with the snow falling,
but there wasn't much blue
in the drifts or corners:
just white and more white
and the sound track so dead
you could almost imagine
the trees were talking.

ADRIEN STOUTENBURG

BALL GAME

Caught off first, he leaped to run to second, but
Then struggled back to first.
He left first because of a natural desire
To leap, to get on with the game.
When you jerk to run to second
You do not necessarily think of a home run.
You want to go on. You want to get to the next stage,
The entire soul is bent on second base.
The fact is that the mind flashes
Faster in action than the muscles can move.
Dramatic! Off first, taut, heading for second,
In a split second, total realization,
Heading for first. Head first! Legs follow fast.
You struggle back to first with victor effort
As, even, after a life of effort and chill,
One flashes back to the safety of childhood,
To that strange place where one had first begun.

RICHARD EBERHART

HORROR MOVIE

Dr. Unlikely, we love you so,
You who made the double-headed rabbits grow
From a single hare. Mutation's friend,
Who could have prophecied the end
When the Spider Woman deftly snared the fly
And the monsters strangled in a monstrous kiss
And somebody hissed, "You'll hang for this!"?

Dear Dracula, sleeping on your native soil,
(Any other kind makes him spoil),
How we clapped when you broke the French door down
And surprised the bride in the overwrought bed.
Perfectly dressed for lunar research,
Your evening cape added much,
Though the bride, inexplicably dressed in furs,
Was a study in jaded jugulars.

Poor, tortured Leopard Man, you changed your spots
In the debauched village of the Pin-Head Tots;
How we wrung our hands, how we wept
When the eighteenth murder proved inept,
And, caught in the Phosphorous Cave of Sea,
Dangling the last of synthetic flesh,
You said, "There's something wrong with me."

The Wolf Man knew when he prowled at dawn
Beginnings spin a web where endings spawn.
The bat who lived on shaving cream,
A household pet of Dr. Dream,
Unfortunately, maddened by the bedlam,
Turned on the Doc, bit the hand that fed him.

And you, Dr. X, who killed by moonlight,
We loved your scream in the laboratory
When the panel slid and the night was starry
And you threw the inventor in the crocodile pit
(An obscure point: Did he deserve it?)
And you took the gold to Transylvania
Where no one guessed how insane you were.

We thank you for the moral and the mood,
Dear Dr. Cliché, Nurse Platitude.
When we meet again by the Overturned Grave,
Near the Sunken City of the Twisted Mind,
(In The Son of the Son of Frankenstein),
Make the blood flow, make the motive muddy:
There's a little death in every body.

HOWARD MOSS

JUMP SHOT

Lithe, quicker than the ball itself;
Spinning through the blocking forearms,
Hands like stars, spread to suspend
The ball from five, and only five,
Magic fingerprints.

The rebound resounding down the pole
And into asphalt, pounded hard by sneakers
Raggedier than the missing-tooth grimaces.

Grimaces. No smiles here. Concentration.
Movement. The calculation.
The arch-back leap. And off the rim again.
Once in ten the satisfying swoosh.

And no time wasted to enjoy it.
Grasp that globe and keep it dribbling:
Elbows were meant for eyesockets;
Work it up higher than hands,
Higher than the grab of gravity.

Working, each man for himself,
Yet neatly, neatly weaving in the pattern.

RICHARD PECK

THE HIGH SCHOOL BAND

On warm days in September the high school band
Is up with the birds and marches along our street,
Boom boom,
To a field where it goes boom boom until eight forty-five
When it marches, as in the old rhyme, back, boom boom,
To its study halls, leaving our street
Empty except for the leaves that descend, to no drum,
And lie still.
In September
A great many high school bands beat a great many drums,
And the silences after their partings are very deep.

REED WHITTEMORE

THE WORLD IS A BEAUTIFUL PLACE

The world is a beautiful place
to be born into
if you don't mind happiness
not always being
so very much fun
if you don't mind a touch of hell
now and then
just when everything is fine
because even in heaven
they don't sing
all the time
The world is a beautiful place
to be born into
if you don't mind some people dying
all the time
or maybe only starving
some of the time
which isn't half so bad
if it isn't you.

LAWRENCE FERLINGHETTI

THE BRICK BENCH OUTSIDE THE HOUSE

TO MY BROTHER MIGUEL:
In Memoriam

Brother, today I sit on the brick bench outside the
house,
where you make a bottomless emptiness.
I remember we used to play at this hour of the day,
and mama
would calm us: "There now, boys . . ."

Now I go hide
as before, from all these evening
prayers, and I hope that you will not find me.
In the parlor, the entrance hall, the corridors.
Later, you hide, and I do not find you.
I remember we made each other cry,
brother, in that game.

Miguel, you hid yourself
one night in August, nearly at daybreak,
but instead of laughing when you hid, you were sad.
And your other heart of those dead afternoons
is tired of looking and not finding you. And now
shadows fall on the soul.

Listen, brother, don't be too late
coming out. All right? Mama might worry.

CESAR VALLEJO
(TRANSLATED BY JOHN KNOEPFLE AND JAMES WRIGHT)

THE WHIPPING

The old woman across the way
  is whipping the boy again
and shouting to the neighborhood
  her goodness and his wrongs.

Wildly he crashes through elephant ears,
  pleads in dusty zinnias,
while she in spite of crippling fat
  pursues and corners him.

She strikes and strikes the shrilly circling
  boy till the stick breaks
in her hand. His tears are rainy weather
  to woundlike memories:

My head gripped in bony vise
  of knees, the writhing struggle

to wrench free, the blows, the fear
  worse than blows that hateful

Words could bring, the face that I
  no longer knew or loved . . .
Well, it is over now, it is over,
  and the boy sobs in his room,

And the woman leans muttering against
  a tree, exhausted, purged—
avenged in part for lifelong hidings
  she has had to bear.

ROBERT HAYDEN

AT 79TH AND PARK

A cry!—someone is knocked
Down on the avenue;
People don't know what to do
When a walker lies, not breathing.

I watch, ten storeys high,
Through the acetylene air:
He has been backed-up over;
Still, the accident

Is hard to credit. A group
Of 14 gathers; the Fire
Department rains like bees,
Visored, black-striped on yellow

Batting, buzz—they clamber
Around that globule; somebody
Brings out a comforter
For shroud; a woman's puce

Scarf bobs, from my 10th-floor view,
Desperately; by the backed truck
An arm explains, hacks air
In desperation, though no

One takes much notice. As through
A pail of glass, I see—
Far down—an ambulance,
A doctor come; they slide

Away the stretcher. . . . In minutes
The piston-arm, the truck,
Puce, police, bees, group
All have been vacuumed up.

BARBARA HOWES

WHEN MAHALIA SINGS

We used to gather at the high window
of the holiness church and, on tip-toe,
look in and laugh at the dresses, too small
on the ladies, and how wretched they all
looked—an old garage for a church, for pews,
old wooden chairs. It seemed a lame excuse
for a church. Not solemn or grand,
with no real robed choir, but a loose jazz band,
or so it sounded to our mocking ears.
So we responded to their hymns with jeers.

Sometimes those holiness people would dance,
and this we knew sprang from deep ignorance
of how to rightly worship God, who after
all was pleased not by such foolish laughter
but by the stiffly still hands in our church
where we saw no one jump or shout or lurch
or weep. We laughed to hear those holiness
rhythms making a church a song fest:
we heard this music as the road to sin,
down which they traveled toward that end.

I, since then, have heard the gospel singing
of one who says I worship with clapping
hands and my whole body, God, whom we must
thank for all this richness raised from dust.
Seeing her high-thrown head reminded
me of those holiness high-spirited,
who like angels, like saints, worshiped as whole
men with rhythm, with dance, with singing soul.
Since then, I've learned of my familiar God—
He finds no worship alien or odd.

QUANDRA PRETTYMAN

AMERICAN RHAPSODY (4)

First you bite your fingernails. And then you comb your hair
again. And then you wait. And wait.
(They say, you know, that first you lie. And then you steal, they
say. And then, they say, you kill.)

Then the doorbell rings. Then Peg drops in. And Bill. And Jane.
And Doc.
And first you talk, and smoke, and hear the news and have a
drink. Then you walk down the stairs.
And you dine, then, and go to a show after that, perhaps, and
after that a night spot, and after that come home again, and
climb the stairs again, and again go to bed.

But first Peg argues, and Doc replies. First you dance the same
dance and you drink the same drink you always drank
before.
And the piano builds a roof of notes above the world.

And the trumpet weaves a dome of music through space. And the
drum makes a ceiling over space and time and night.
And then the table-wit. And then the check. Then home again to
bed.
But first the stairs.

And do you now, baby, as you climb the stairs, do you still feel
as you felt back there?
Do you feel again as you felt this morning? And the night
before? And then the night before that?
(They say, you know, that first you hear voices. And then you
have visions, they say. Then, they say, you kick and scream
and rave.)

Or do you feel: What is one more night in a lifetime of nights?
What is one more death, or friendship, or divorce out of two, or
three? Or four? Or five?
One more face among so many, many faces, or one more life
among so many million lives?
But first, baby, as you climb and count the stairs (and they total
the same) did you, sometime or somewhere, have a different
idea?
Is this, baby, what you were born to feel, and do, and be?

KENNETH FEARING

MODIFICATIONS

When I was young and we were poor and I used to
gripe about the food, my mother would say
"Eat what's in front of you and be thankful you

ain't worse off." That didn't make much of an
impression then and after I left home I didn't
think any more about it except to make fun,

you know how that goes. Then a few months ago
I had a lot of trouble, nothing that most
people couldn't handle but I'm not most people

and it wigged me out all but for good. The
only way I held my junk-shop life together was
by remembering all the good old rules: So now

I honor my father and mother like crazy, go to
bed really early, take hundreds of stitches
in time but most of all I eat what's put in front

of me. Lately I've eaten a lot of forks and
things and right now there's a nice waitress in the
hospital just because she didn't move her hand in

time. It's too bad but I've just got to have the
rules to keep my arms and legs from flying off, so
whenever I sit down I think them over and chew 50

times and say thank you thank you thank you thank
you thank you thank you thank you thank you thank
you thank you thank you thank you thank you.

RON KOERTGE

HE DON'T KNOW THE INSIDE *FEEL*

My teacher fish!
You must be screwed up, man.
A teacher? Hell
A teacher TEACHES.
He don't know the outdoor stuff.
He don't care.
He'd never walk by himself
Before breakfast
Across fields
Gettin his feet soaked
Just to fish!
He's a teacher.
He teaches.

He marks papers
Or he reads books.
He don't fish with no 2-ounce rod
And lay that long line easy on the top
Like this here . . . Look!
Oh, man
Don't tell me he hears them wild birds.
He don't.
He don't know the *inside* feel
Of white water rushin
Cold against his knees.
He don't know fishin, man.
Not like me.

HERBERT R. ADAMS

teechur

he is trying to think
                    to teach them to think
he tries it by a pond
to tell them why he likes it
to help them like it

he teaches them
he makes love to them
he dies with them a little

they ask no questions

after a while they all go away

DICK HIGGINS

FREEDOM IS FOLLOWING A RIVER

FREEDOM

Freedom is not following a river.
Freedom is following a river,
  though, if you want to.
It is deciding now by what happens now.
It is knowing that luck makes a difference.

No leader is free; no follower is free—
  the rest of us can often be free.
Most of the world are living by
creeds too odd, chancey, and habit-forming
  to be worth arguing about by reason.

If you are oppressed, wake up about
four in the morning: most places,
you can usually be free some of the time
  if you wake up before other people.

WILLIAM STAFFORD

ONCE I PASS'D THROUGH A POPULOUS CITY

Once I pass'd through a populous city imprinting my brain for
future use with its shows, architecture, customs, traditions,
Yet now of all that city I remember only a woman I casually met
there who detain'd me for love of me,
Day by day and night by night we were together—all else has
long been forgotten by me,
I remember I say only that woman who passionately clung to me,
Again we wander, we love, we separate again,
Again she holds me by the hand, I must not go,
I see her close beside me with silent lips sad and tremulous.

WALT WHITMAN

TRANSCONTINENT

Where the cities end, the
dumps grow the oil-can shacks
from Portland, Maine,

to Seattle. Broken
cars rust in Troy, New York,
and Cleveland Heights.

On the train, the people
eat candy bars, and watch,
or fall asleep.

When they look outside and
see cars and shacks, they know
they're nearly there.

DONALD HALL

WIRES

The widest prairies have electric fences,
For though old cattle know they must not stray,
Young steers are always scenting purer water
Not here but anywhere. Beyond the wires

Leads them to blunder up against the wires
Whose muscle-shredding violence gives no quarter.
Young steers become old cattle from that day,
Electric limits to their wildest senses.

PHILIP LARKIN

BUFFALO DUSK

The buffaloes are gone.
And those who saw the buffaloes are gone.
Those who saw the buffaloes by thousands and
  how they pawed the prairie sod into dust
  with their hoofs, their great heads down
  pawing on in a great pageant of dusk,
Those who saw the buffaloes are gone.
And the buffaloes are gone.

CARL SANDBURG

OLD DOLORES

In the country down below,
Where the little piñons grow
And it's nearly always half a day to water,
There used to stand a town
Where a crick came tumblin' down
From a mesa where she surely hadn't oughter.

The streets were bright with candlelight,
The whole town joined the chorus,
And every man in sight let his cattle drift at night
Just to mosey to the town of Old Dolores.

Then things would kinda spin
Till the sun come up again
Like the back of some old yeller prairie wagon
And show us, dim and red,
Maybe half a hundred head
Of our saddle ponies standin', reins a-draggin'.

The red brick walls, the waterfalls,
The whole wide world before us—

But the dobe walls are gone, and the goat bells in the dawn
Ain't a-jinglin' in the streets of Old Dolores.

The Greaser girls would fool
On the plaza in the cool,
And there's one I used to meet her by a willow,
But I guess that any girl
Makes a fellow's head to whirl
When the same's been usin' saddles for a pillow.

The wide-eyed stars, the long cigars,
The smiles that waited for us!
If there's any little well down inside the gates of hell,
Then I know the boys have named it "Old Dolores."

ANONYMOUS
(*Traditional Western song*)

COWBOY SONG

I come from Salem County
  Where the silver melons grow,
Where the wheat is sweet as an angel's feet
  And the zithering zephyrs blow.
I walk the blue bone-orchard
  In the apple-blossom snow,
Where the teasy bees take their honeyed ease
  And the marmalade moon hangs low.

My maw sleeps prone on the prairie
  In a boulder eiderdown,
Where the pickled stars in their little jam-jars
  Hang in a hoop to town.
I haven't seen paw since a Sunday
  In eighteen seventy-three
When he packed his snap in a bitty mess-trap
  And said he'd be home by tea.

Fled is my fancy sister
  All weeping like the willow,
And dead is the brother I loved like no other
  Who once did share my pillow.
I fly the florid water
  Where run the seven geese round,

O the townsfolk talk to see me walk
  Six inches off the ground.

Across the map of midnight
  I trawl the turning sky,
In my green glass the salt fleets pass
  The moon her fire-float by.
The girls go gay in the valley
  When the boys come down from the farm,
Don't run, my joy, from a poor cowboy,
  I won't do you no harm.

The bread of my twentieth birthday
  I buttered with the sun,
Though I sharpen my eyes with lovers' lies
  I'll never see twenty-one.
Light is my shirt with lilies,
  And lined with lead my hood,
On my face as I pass is a plate of brass,
  And my suit is made of wood.

CHARLES CAUSLEY

STAYING ALIVE

Staying alive in the woods is a matter of calming down
At first and deciding whether to wait for rescue,
Trusting to others,
Or simply to start walking and walking in one direction
Till you come out—or something happens to stop you.
By far the safer choice
Is to settle down where you are, and try to make a living
Off the land, camping near water, away from shadows.
Eat no white berries;
Spit out all bitterness. Shooting at anything
Means hiking further and further every day
To hunt survivors;
It may be best to learn what you have to learn without a gun,
Not killing but watching birds and animals go
In and out of shelter
At will. Following their example, build for a whole season:
Facing across the wind in your lean-to,
You may feel wilder,
And nothing, not even you, will have to stay in hiding.
If you have no matches, a stick and a fire-bow
Will keep you warmer,
Or the crystal of your watch, filled with water, held up to the sun
Will do the same, in time. In case of snow,
Drifting toward winter,
Don't try to stay awake through the night, afraid of freezing—

The bottom of your mind knows all about zero;
It will turn you over
And shake you till you waken. If you have trouble sleeping
Even in the best of weather, jumping to follow
The unidentifiable noises of the night and feeling
Bears and packs of wolves nuzzling your elbow,
Remember the trappers
Who treated them indifferently and were left alone.
If you hurt yourself, no one will comfort you
Or take your temperature,
So stumbling, wading, and climbing are as dangerous as flying.
But if you decide, at last, you must break through
In spite of all danger,
Think of yourself by time and not by distance, counting
Wherever you're going by how long it takes you;
No other measure
Will bring you safe to nightfall. Follow no streams: they run
Under the ground or fall into wilder country.
Remember the stars
And moss when your mind runs into circles. If it should rain,
Or the fog should roll the horizon in around you,
Hold still for hours
Or days, if you must, or weeks, for seeing is believing
In the wilderness. And if you find a pathway,
Wheel rut, or fence wire,

Retrace it left or right—someone knew where he was going
Once upon a time, and you can follow
Hopefully, somewhere,
Just in case. There may even come, on some uncanny evening,
A time when you're warm and dry, well fed, not thirsty,
Uninjured, without fear,
When nothing, either good or bad, is happening.
This is called staying alive. It's temporary.
What occurs after
Is doubtful. You must always be ready for something to come
bursting
Through the far edge of a clearing, running toward you,
Grinning from ear to ear
And hoarse with welcome. Or something crossing and hovering
Overhead, as light as air, like a break in the sky,
Wondering what you are.
Here you are face to face with the problem of recognition.
Having no time to make smoke, too much to say,
You should have a mirror
With a tiny hole in the back for better aiming, for reflecting
Whatever disaster you can think of, to show
The way you suffer.
These body signals have universal meaning: If you are lying
Flat on your back with arms outstretched behind you,

You say you require
Emergency treatment; if you are standing erect and holding
Arms horizontal, you mean you are not ready;
If you hold them over
Your head, you want to be picked up. Three of anything
Is a sign of distress. Afterward, if you see
No ropes, no ladders,
No maps or messages falling, no searchlights or trails blazing,
Then chances are, you should be prepared to burrow
Deep for a deep winter.

DAVID WAGONER

THE MOTORCYCLIST'S SONG
(In Mexico City)

That blacksnake across the furrows
        of America
north, that sweet road,
where the cycle breathes
                all the far-off lights,
and the sun glints in the gaunt corn,
   Ohio.

That patient necklace North,
where streetlights crowd
   the midnight streets,
and the hick-towns bob
        like beads,
all on the same black thread.

Guitar-string of a road!
sing me Wurlitzer cafés
        fluorescent even at dawn.

(Ah! North, sweet necklace,
        spin me soon,
where the lighthouses scribe
        the sea—
my love counts the stars
        with her green eyes,
and wants no other but me.)

DEWITT BELL

THE STRONG MEN KEEP COMING ON

UPSTREAM

The strong men keep coming on.
They go down shot, hanged, sick, broken.
They live on fighting, singing, lucky as plungers.
The strong mothers pulling them on. . . .
The strong mothers pulling them from a dark sea, a great
prairie, a long mountain.
Call hallelujah, call amen, call deep thanks.
The strong men keep coming on.

CARL SANDBURG

HUNGER

The skiing champs
cling together
in groups

they are
masters they know
how to turn

the turns
shave the slalom poles
close to the 100th

of a second
with a brutal
elegance.

The admirers
hustle below
click the times

throw enamored glances
at the idols who discuss
the others' impossible style.

The competing teams
shake heads all day
at the position

of the hips
of the adversaries
as they race

down the slopes
the turns
turn out alike

and new snow
covers the tracks
in the night

of their victory
banquet.

LENNART BRUCE

THIEF JONES

The people living round the place
Called him Thief Jones to his face,
Thief was like a Christian name,
It had lost the smut of shame.
Thief's house was black and let in weather,
The ridgepole hardly held together,
The doorway stood at a lee-lurch.
Men often opened it to search
Among the litter of net-corks there
For a lobster-buoy or pair
Of missing pants whose seat was sewn
With patches they could prove their own.
It got so, when a man lost track
Of anything, he took a tack
Down Thief's way and had a look.
The folks at Mundy's Landing took
Thief as they took foggy weather;
They'd learned to get on well together.

Thief never said a word if he
Happened to be in. He'd be
Glad to see the man and might
Help him straighten things out right—
"This rudder's yours, this anchor's mine."
He might invite the man to dine
On the hasty-pudding cooking
On his stove, after the looking.
Men liked to talk with Thief, he knew
Stories yellow, pink, and blue.
But though they liked to hear him lie,
They never halved a blueberry pie
From his cookstove's warming-shelf,
Thief ate his victuals by himself.

ROBERT P. TRISTRAM COFFIN

MR. FLOOD'S PARTY

Old Eben Flood, climbing alone one night
Over the hill between the town below
And the forsaken upland hermitage
That held as much as he should ever know
On earth again of home, paused warily.
The road was his with not a native near;
And Eben, having leisure, said aloud,
For no man else in Tilbury Town to hear:

"Well, Mr. Flood, we have the harvest moon
Again, and we may not have many more;
The bird is on the wing, the poet says,
And you and I have said it here before.
Drink to the bird." He raised up to the light
The jug that he had gone so far to fill,
And answered huskily: "Well, Mr. Flood,
Since you propose it, I believe I will."

Alone, as if enduring to the end
A valiant armor of scarred hopes outworn,
He stood there in the middle of the road
Like Roland's ghost winding a silent horn.
Below him, in the town among the trees,
Where friends of other days had honored him,

A phantom salutation of the dead
Rang thinly till old Eben's eyes were dim.

Then, as a mother lays her sleeping child
Down tenderly, fearing it may awake,
He set the jug down slowly at his feet
With trembling care, knowing that most things break;
And only when assured that on firm earth
It stood, as the uncertain lives of men
Assuredly did not, he paced away,
And with his hand extended paused again:

"Well, Mr. Flood, we have not met like this
In a long time; and many a change has come
To both of us, I fear, since last it was
We had a drop together. Welcome home!"
Convivially returning with himself,
Again he raised the jug up to the light;
And with an acquiescent quaver said:
"Well, Mr. Flood, if you insist, I might.

"Only a very little, Mr. Flood—
For auld lang syne. No more, sir; that will do."
So, for the time, apparently it did,
And Eben evidently thought so too;
For soon amid the silver loneliness
Of night he lifted up his voice and sang,

Secure, with only two moons listening,
Until the whole harmonious landscape rang—

"Fur auld lang syne." The weary throat gave out,
The last word wavered; and the song being done,
He raised again the jug regretfully
And shook his head, and was again alone.
There was not much that was ahead of him,
And there was nothing in the town below—
Where strangers would have shut the many doors
That many friends had opened long ago.

EDWIN ARLINGTON ROBINSON

THE RUNNER

On a flat road runs the well-train'd runner,
He is lean and sinewy with muscular legs,
He is thinly clothed, he leans forward as he runs,
With lightly closed fists and arms partially rais'd.

WALT WHITMAN

THE ROAD ALL RUNNERS COME

THE OLD MEN ADMIRING THEMSELVES IN THE WATER

I heard the old, old men say,
"Everything alters,
And one by one we drop away."
They had hands like claws, and their knees
Were twisted like the old thorn-trees
By the waters.
I heard the old, old men say,
"All that's beautiful drifts away
Like the waters."

W. B. YEATS

TO AN ATHLETE DYING YOUNG

The time you won your town the race
We chaired you through the market place;
Man and boy stood cheering by,
And home we brought you shoulder-high.

Today, the road all runners come,
Shoulder-high we bring you home,
And set you at your threshold down,
Townsman of a stiller town.

Smart lad, to slip betimes away
From fields where glory does not stay
And early though the laurel grows
It withers quicker than the rose.

Eyes the shady night has shut
Cannot see the record cut,
And silence sounds no worse than cheers
After earth has stopped the ears:

Now you will not swell the rout
Of lads that wore their honors out,
Runners whom renown outran
And the name died before the man.

So set, before its echoes fade,
The fleet foot on the sill of shade,
And hold to the low lintel up
The still-defended challenge-cup.

And round that early-laureled head
Will flock to gaze the strengthless dead,
And find unwithered on its curls
The garland briefer than a girl's.

A. E. HOUSMAN

EX-BASKETBALL PLAYER

Pearl Avenue runs past the high-school lot,
Bends with the trolley tracks, and stops, cut off
Before it has a chance to go two blocks,
At Colonel McComsky Plaza. Berth's Garage
Is on the corner facing west, and there,
Most days, you'll find Flick Webb, who helps Berth out.

Flick stands tall among the idiot pumps—
Five on a side, the old bubble-head style,
Their rubber elbows hanging loose and low.
One's nostrils are two S's, and his eyes
An E and O. And one is squat, without
A head at all—more of a football type.

Once Flick played for the high-school team, the Wizards.
He was good: in fact, the best. In '46
He bucketed three hundred ninety points,
A county record still. The ball loved Flick.
I saw him rack up thirty-eight or forty
In one home game. His hands were like wild birds.

He never learned a trade, he just sells gas,
Checks oil, and changes flats. Once in a while,
As a gag, he dribbles an inner tube,
But most of us remember anyway.
His hands are fine and nervous on the lug wrench.
It makes no difference to the lug wrench, though.

Off work, he hangs around Mae's Luncheonette.
Grease-grey and kind of coiled, he plays pinball,
Sips lemon cokes, and smokes those thin cigars;
Flick seldom speaks to Mae, just sits and nods
Beyond her face towards bright applauding tiers
Of Necco Wafers, Nibs, and Juju Beads.

JOHN UPDIKE

RICHARD CORY

Whenever Richard Cory went down town,
  We people on the pavement looked at him:
He was a gentleman from sole to crown,
  Clean favored, and imperially slim.

And he was always quietly arrayed,
  And he was always human when he talked;
But still he fluttered pulses when he said,
  "Good-morning," and he glittered when he walked.

And he was rich—yes, richer than a king,
  And admirably schooled in every grace:
In fine, we thought that he was everything
  To make us wish that we were in his place.

So on we worked, and waited for the light,
  And went without the meat, and cursed the bread;
And Richard Cory, one calm summer night,
  Went home and put a bullet through his head.

EDWIN ARLINGTON ROBINSON

ON HURRICANE JACKSON

Now his nose's bridge is broken, one eye
will not focus and the other is a stray;
trainers whisper in his mouth while one ear
listens to itself, clenched like a fist;
generally shadow-boxing in a smoky room,
his mind hides like the aching boys
who lost a contest in the Pan-Hellenic games
and had to take the back roads home,
but someone else, his perfect youth,
laureled in newsprint and dollar bills,
triumphs forever on the great white way
to the statistical Sparta of the champs.

ALAN DUGAN

THE LOSER

and the next I remembered I'm on a table,
everybody's gone: the head of bravery
under light, scowling, flailing me down . . .
and then some toad stood there, smoking a cigar:
"Kid you're no fighter," he told me,
and I got up and knocked him over a chair;
it was like a scene in a movie, and
he stayed there on his big rump and said
over and over: "Jesus, Jesus, whatsamatta wit
you?" and I got up and dressed,
the tape still on my hands, and when I got home
I tore the tape off my hands and
wrote my first poem,
and I've been fighting
ever since.

CHARLES BUKOWSKI

THE VANITY OF HUMAN WISHES

at 16
I dreamed of
a bushy beard
and purple Ford
                    souped up deuce
                    4 on the floor
able to outrun
any cop alive

or drifting
change in my jeans
from town to town
wowing the girls
                            bad man
James Dean back from the dead
Brando on a
hog

16
and here I am at 26 teaching English
not even
              a mustachio
to tickle my wife

JOHN LEAX

COWBOYS: ONE

Brave
they straddle the animals,
hearts racing before the pistol sings
then leaping from the chute
man and animal as one
wedded groin to back.

One small moment in the air
and then the mud.

Hats retrieved
Levis dusted
back to the bull pen
to wait the next event.

Sundays choirboys
in cowboy hats.

COWBOYS: TWO

Huddled in the pits
below the grandstand
or lining at the telephone
to call home victories
they make a gentle picture.
Their billfolds bulging just enough
to make another entrance fee.

Next week Omaha or Dallas.
San Antonio is yet to come.
And now the Cheyenne autumn
  like a golden thread
ties them till the weekend's done.

COWBOYS: THREE

They wade through beer cans
piled ankle high in gutters—
the rodeo has moved
  down from the fairground
to the town
and every hotel door's ajar.
Better than the Mardi Gras.
The nights are longer than Alaska now
until the main event begins
  another afternoon.

But after all the Main Event is still to be
a cowboy
For ten minutes or ten years, it's all the same.
You don't forget the Levis
  hugging you all day
and Stetson hats checked in passing windows
cocked a certain way.

ROD MCKUEN

EPITAPH ON A TYRANT

Perfection, of a kind, was what he was after,
And the poetry he invented was easy to understand;
He knew human folly like the back of his hand,
And was greatly interested in armies and fleets;
When he laughed, respectable senators burst with laughter,
And when he cried the little children died in the streets.

W. H. AUDEN

BOWERY

Bums are the spirit of us parked in
ratty old hotels.
Bums are what we have made of
angels,
given them old clothes to wear
dirty beards and an alcoholic breath,
to lie sprawled on gutters at our feet
as sacrifices to our idols: power and
money.

Bums ask themselves, Why dress and
shave,
and be well mannered, studious and
hard-working,
own homes and debts, a bank account
and business
friends when others more eager are
doing it
successfully? All we want is the right
to sit propped up against a wall,
drunk

and drooling, letting urine seep
    through
our clothes onto the sidewalk, we
unconscious or unconcerned.
                    We with no money
relax anyway, letting the world
    come in
on us in sidewalk spit on which we
    sprawl,
in kicks and jabs from cops, under
    open skies
in rain and snow. None of you dares
    do it,
and so you do not know what money
    means.
We who live on charity enjoy the
    pleasure
of your wealth, the long hours filled
with drunkenness.

DAVID IGNATOW

I'LL MAKE ME A WORLD

THE OLD REPAIR MAN

God is the Old Repair Man.
When we are junk in Nature's storehouse
    he takes us apart.
What is good he lays aside; he might use it some day.
What has decayed he buries in six feet of sod
    to nurture the weeds.
Those we leave behind moisten the sod with their tears;
But their eyes are blind as to where he has placed
    the good.
Some day the Old Repair Man
Will take the good from its secret place
And with his gentle, strong hands will mold
A more enduring work—a work that will defy Nature—
And we will laugh at the old days, the troubled days,
When we were but a crude piece of craftsmanship,
When we were but an experiment in Nature's
    laboratory . . .
It is good we have the Old Repair Man.

FENTON JOHNSON

THE CREATION

And God stepped out on space,
And He looked around and said:
I'm lonely—
I'll make me a world.

And far as the eye of God could see
Darkness covered everything,
Blacker than a hundred midnights
Down in a cypress swamp.

Then God smiled,
And the light broke,
And the darkness rolled up on one side,
And the light stood shining on the other,
And God said: That's good!

Then God reached out and took the light in His hands,
And God rolled the light around in His hands
Until He made the sun;

And He set that sun a-blazing in the heavens.
And the light that was left from making the sun
God gathered it up in a shining ball
And flung it against the darkness,
Spangling the night with the moon and stars.
Then down between
The darkness and the light

He hurled the world;
And God said: That's good!

Then God himself stepped down—
And the sun was on His right hand,
And the moon was on His left;
The stars were clustered about His head,
And the earth was under His feet.
And God walked, and where He trod
His footsteps hollowed the valleys out
And bulged the mountains up.

Then He stopped and looked and saw
That the earth was hot and barren.
So God stepped over to the edge of the world
And He spat out the seven seas—
He batted His eyes, and the lightnings flashed—
He clapped His hands, and the thunders rolled—
And the waters above the earth came down,
The cooling waters came down.

Then the green grass sprouted,
And the little red flowers blossomed,
The pine tree pointed his finger to the sky,
And the oak spread out his arms,
The lakes cuddled down in the hollows of the ground,
And the rivers ran down to the sea;
And God smiled again,

And the rainbow appeared,
And curled itself around His shoulder.

Then God raised His arm and He waved His hand
Over the sea and over the land,
And He said: Bring forth! Bring forth!
And quicker than God could drop His hand,
Fishes and fowls
And beasts and birds
Swam the rivers and the seas,
Roamed the forests and the woods,
And split the air with their wings.
And God said: That's good!

Then God walked around,
And God looked around
On all that He had made.
He looked at His sun,
And He looked at His moon,
And He looked at His little stars;
He looked on His world
With all its living things,
And God said: I'm lonely still.

Then God sat down—
On the side of a hill where He could think;
By a deep, wide river He sat down;
With His head on His hands,
God thought and thought,
Till He thought: I'll make me a man!

Up from the bed of the river
God scooped the clay;
And by the bank of the river
He kneeled Him down;
And there the great God Almighty
Who lit the sun and fixed it in the sky,
Who flung the stars to the most far corner of the night,
Who rounded the earth in the middle of His hand;
This Great God,
Like a mammy bending over her baby,
Kneeled down in the dust
Toiling over a lump of clay
Till He shaped it in His own image;

Then into it He blew the breath of life,
And man became a living soul.
Amen. Amen.

JAMES WELDON JOHNSON

FUELED

Fueled
by a million
man-made
wings of fire—
the rocket tore a tunnel
through the sky—
and everybody cheered.
Fueled
only by a thought from God—
the seedling
urged its way
through thicknesses of black—
and as it pierced
the heavy ceiling of the soil—
and launched itself
up into outer space—
no
one
even
clapped.

MARCIE HANS

THE STUMP

Today they cut down the oak.
Strong men climbed with ropes
in the brittle tree.
The exhaust of a gasoline saw
was blue in the branches.

It is February. The oak has been dead a year.
I remember the great sails of its branches
rolling out greenly, a hundred and twenty feet up,
and acorns thick on the lawn.
Nine cities of squirrels lived in that tree.
Today they run over the snow
squeaking their lamentation.

Yet I was happy that it was coming down.
"Let it come down!" I kept saying to myself
with a joy that was strange to me.
Though the oak was the shade of old summers,
I loved the guttural saw.

DONALD HALL

FABLE FOR WHEN THERE'S NO WAY OUT

Grown too big for his skin,
and it grown hard,

without a sea and atmosphere—
he's drunk it all up—

his strength's inside him now,
but there's no room to stretch.

He pecks at the top
but his beak's too soft;

though instinct and ambition shoves,
he can't get through.

Barely old enough to bleed
and already bruised!

In a case this tough
what's the use

if you break your head
instead of the lid?

Despair tempts him
to just go limp:

Maybe the cell's
already a tomb,

and beginning end
in this round room.

Still, stupidly he pecks
and pecks, as if from under

his own skull—
yet makes no crack . . .

No crack until
he finally cracks,

and kicks and stomps.
What a thrill

and shock to feel
his little gaff poke

through the floor!
A way he hadn't known or meant.

Rage works if reason won't.
When locked up, bear down.

MAY SWENSON

EARTH

If this little world tonight
  Suddenly should fall through space
In a hissing, headlong flight,
  Shriveling from off its face,
As it falls into the sun,
  In an instant every trace
Of the little crawling things—
Ants, philosophers, and lice,
Cattle, cockroaches, and kings,
  Beggars, millionaires, and mice,
Men and maggots all as one
As it falls into the sun. . . .
Who can say but at the same
  Instant from some planet far
A child may watch us and exclaim:
  "See the pretty shooting star!"

OLIVER HERFORD

SUMMER HOLIDAY

When the sun shouts and people abound
One thinks there were the ages of stone and the age of bronze
And the iron age; iron the unstable metal;
Steel made of iron, unstable as his mother; the towered-up cities
Will be stains of rust on mounds of plaster.
Roots will not pierce the heaps for a time, kind rains will cure
   them,
Then nothing will remain of the iron age
And all these people but a thigh-bone or so, a poem
Stuck in the world's thought, splinters of glass
In the rubbish dumps, a concrete dam far off in the
   mountain . . .

ROBINSON JEFFERS

MISSION UNCONTROLLED

They left him behind
on some subsequent moonshot.
Un-of course-intentionally:
the quick pull-out lift-off,
due to a readily identifiable
tube-flicker, everyone agreeing later:
correctable.

Caught in the updraft of that sudden rising,
he turned toward earth no longer at his feet:
agate in onyx, and setting.

Wondering at his fate, his luck,
he began a natural wheezing,
before the imported air played out—
slowly it ebbed like lilac—
creating little saturns near the goggles,
coloring the moon.

Time still to step
in ovoid spoor where
aerolites had bounced before,
tracking, stalking a little
before the inevitable sinking-to-the-knees.

Then, on moon level, fingers drumming
the surface, dancing away, half-
captivated by second-rate gravity,

he began to dig . . . like any animal thing
too far from the cave.

Dust gave way to gravel
and in a little finger-funnel
just at the last gasp, so to speak,
he turned it up:
an arrowhead.

RICHARD PECK

DREAM VARIATION

To fling my arms wide
In some place of the sun,
To whirl and to dance
Till the white day is done.
Then rest at cool evening
Beneath a tall tree
While night comes on gently,
  Dark like me—
That is my dream!

To fling my arms wide
In the face of the sun,
Dance! Whirl! Whirl!
Till the quick day is done.
Rest at pale evening . . .
A tall, slim tree . . .
Night coming tenderly
  Black like me.

LANGSTON HUGHES

A DESIGN OF WHITE BONES

THE DEATH OF THE SPORTS-CAR DRIVER

German steel built like a water-drop
Is burning, silver still, upon its top.
Pirelli tires turn against the sky
With nothing more to match their rubber by
Than a worn-out king-pin that snapped and sent
Its servant spinning in a farmer's harvest.

Dry leaves are fired. This my father did
In corduroys and silence. Overhead
Geese echeloned for warmth out of this world
That stirred my bedtime when I was a child.
I wonder what I can remember means.
What's yelling to be let out of my chest?

Some farmers dressed in jackets to their knees
Come slowly through the birch and maple trees.
Crows spell up from their colored cupolas
And leave me to the wreckage of their caws.
When I am found, what will the crying sound like?
I have no orders for my little man.

My heart is where my heart's supposed to be,
And soon it will explode inside of me—
Blue flame! Now I am rubber, steel, and heat,
And the three of me rise smoking to repeat
Ourselves. This is a countryside of ghosts.
I wreck the world with the dream of my disaster.

JONATHAN AARON

BETWEEN THE WORLD AND ME

And one morning while in the woods I stumbled
suddenly upon the thing.
Stumbled upon it in a grassy clearing guarded by scaly
oaks and elms.
And the sooty details of the scene rose, thrusting
themselves between the world and me. . . .

There was a design of white bones slumbering
forgottenly upon a cushion of ashes.
There was a charred stump of a sapling pointing a blunt
finger accusingly at the sky.
There were torn tree limbs, tiny veins of burnt leaves,
and a scorched coil of greasy hemp;
A vacant shoe, an empty tie, a ripped shirt, a lonely hat,
and a pair of trousers stiff with black blood.
And upon the trampled grass were buttons, dead
matches, butt-ends of cigars and cigarettes, peanut
shells, a drained gin-flask, and a whore's lipstick;
Scattered traces of tar, restless arrays of feathers, and the
lingering smell of gasoline.
And through the morning air the sun poured yellow
surprise into the eye sockets of a stony skull. . . .
And while I stood my mind was frozen with a cold pity
for the life that was gone.
The ground gripped my feet and my heart was circled
by icy walls of fear—
The sun died in the sky; a night wind muttered in the
grass and fumbled the leaves in the trees; the

woods poured forth the hungry yelping of hounds; the darkness screamed with thirsty voices; and the witnesses rose and lived:

The dry bones stirred, rattled, lifted, melting themselves into my bones.

The grey ashes formed flesh firm and black, entering into my flesh.

The gin-flask passed from mouth to mouth; cigars and cigarettes glowed, the whore smeared the lipstick red upon her lips,

And a thousand faces swirled around me, clamoring that my life be burned. . . .

And then they had me, stripped me, battering my teeth into my throat till I swallowed my own blood.

My voice was drowned in the roar of their voices, and my black wet body slipped and rolled in their hands as they bound me to the sapling.

And my skin clung to the bubbling hot tar, falling from me in limp patches.

And the down and quills of the white feathers sank into my raw flesh, and I moaned in my agony.

Then my blood was cooled mercifully, cooled by a baptism of gasoline.

And in a blaze of red I leaped to the sky as pain rose like water, boiling my limbs.

RICHARD WRIGHT

MALFUNCTION

He fell in a sweeping arc
From airplane to earth.

You could almost express it
In an equation:

Speed of the airplane minus
Force of the propblast,

Pull of gravity, speed and
Direction of wind,

The slight factor of his jump,
Thrust of leg muscle.

I did not witness his fall,
I was too far off,

Too busy trying to slip
Away from the trees,

Pulling the risers, watching
The scallops of silk

Ruffled above by the wind.
I heard distant shouts:

"Pull your reserve! Pull! Reserve!"
I looked below me,

Saw the earth, the discs of chutes
Sliding to the ground

Like cookies off a tin sheet.
After I landed

It was much too far to walk.
I saw men running,

But the trucks were parked this way.
I know he is dead,

Know we will talk about it
Riding in the trucks

Feeling wind in our faces.
By tonight I would

Describe what all will have seen
By then: he fell fast

Without a sound, like a rock
In a handkerchief;

I was close by when he hit,
Saw him bounce six feet.

Forgetting to drink a toast
We will press bottles

Against our faces and hands,
Clinging to coldness,

Reliving all but the slight
Factor of his death.

RICHARD E. ALBERT

FIRE AND ICE

Some say the world will end in fire,
Some say in ice.
From what I've tasted of desire
I hold with those who favor fire.
But if it had to perish twice,
I think I know enough of hate
To say that for destruction ice
Is also great
And would suffice.

ROBERT FROST

THE QUARRY

O what is that sound which so thrills the ear
  Down in the valley drumming, drumming?
Only the scarlet soldiers, dear,
  The soldiers coming.

O what is that light I see flashing so clear
  Over the distance brightly, brightly?
Only the sun on their weapons, dear,
  As they step lightly.

O what are they doing with all that gear,
  What are they doing this morning, this morning?
Only their usual manoeuvres, dear,
  Or perhaps a warning.

O why have they left the road down there,
  Why are they suddenly wheeling, wheeling?
Perhaps a change in their orders, dear.
  Why are you kneeling?

O haven't they stopped for the doctor's care,
  Haven't they reined their horses, their horses?
Why, they are none of them wounded, dear,
  None of these forces.

O is it the parson they want, with white hair,
  Is it the parson, is it, is it?
No, they are passing his gateway, dear,
  Without a visit.

O it must be the farmer who lives so near.
  It must be the farmer so cunning, so cunning?
They have passed the farmyard already, dear,
  And now they are running.

O where are you going? Stay with me here!
  Were the vows you swore deceiving, deceiving?
No, I promised to love you, dear,
  But I must be leaving.

O it's broken the lock and splintered the door,
  O it's the gate where they're turning, turning;
Their boots are heavy on the floor
  And their eyes are burning.

W. H. AUDEN

OUT, OUT—

The buzz saw snarled and rattled in the yard
And made dust and dropped stove-length sticks of wood,
Sweet-scented stuff when the breeze drew across it.
And from there those that lifted eyes could count
Five mountain ranges one behind the other
Under the sunset far into Vermont.
And the saw snarled and rattled, snarled and rattled,
As it ran light, or had to bear a load.
And nothing happened: day was all but done.
Call it a day, I wish they might have said
To please the boy by giving him the half hour
That a boy counts so much when saved from work.
His sister stood beside them in her apron
To tell them "Supper." At the word, the saw,
As if to prove saws knew what supper meant,
Leaped out at the boy's hand, or seemed to leap—
He must have given the hand. However it was,

Neither refused the meeting. But the hand!
The boy's first outcry was a rueful laugh,
As he swung toward them holding up the hand
Half in appeal, but half as if to keep
The life from spilling. Then the boy saw all—
Since he was old enough to know, big boy
Doing a man's work, though a child at heart—
He saw all spoiled. "Don't let him cut my hand off—
The doctor, when he comes. Don't let him, sister!"
So. But the hand was gone already.
The doctor put him in the dark of ether.
He lay and puffed his lips out with his breath.
And then—the watcher at his pulse took fright.
No one believed. They listened at his heart.
Little—less—nothing!—and that ended it.
No one to build on there. And they, since they
Were not the one dead, turned to their affairs.

ROBERT FROST

TRACT

I will teach you my townspeople
how to perform a funeral—
for you have it over a troop
of artists—
unless one should scour the world—
you have the ground sense necessary.

See! the hearse leads.
I begin with a design for a hearse.
For Christ's sake not black—
nor white either—and not polished!
Let it be weathered—like a farm wagon—
with gilt wheels (this could be
applied fresh with small expense)
or no wheels at all:
a rough dray to drag over the ground.

Knock the glass out!
My God—glass, my townspeople!
For what purpose? Is it for the dead
to look out for us to see
how well he is housed or to see
the flowers or the lack of them—
or what?

To keep the rain and snow from him?
He will have a heavier rain soon:
pebbles and dirt and what not.

Let there be no glass—
and no upholstery! phew!
and no little brass rollers
and small easy wheels on the bottom—
my townspeople what are you thinking of!
A rough plain hearse then
with gilt wheels and no top at all.
On this the coffin lies
by its own weight.

No wreaths please—
especially no hot-house flowers!
Some common memento is better,
something he prized and is known by:
his old clothes—a few books perhaps—
God knows what! You realize
how we are about these things,
my townspeople—
something will be found—anything—
even flowers if he had come to that.
So much for the hearse.

For heaven's sake though see to the driver!
Take off the silk hat! In fact
that's no place at all for him
up there unceremoniously
dragging our friend out to his own dignity!
Bring him down—bring him down!
Low and inconspicuous! I'd not have him ride

on the wagon at all—damn him—
the undertaker's understrapper!
Let him hold the reins
and walk at the side
and inconspicuously too!

Then briefly as to yourselves:
Walk behind—as they do in France,
seventh class, or, if you ride,
Hell take curtains! Go with some show
of inconvenience; sit openly—
to the weather as to grief.
Or do you think you can shut grief in?
What—from us? We who have perhaps
nothing to lose? Share with us
share with us—it will be money
in your pockets.

Go now
I think you are ready.

WILLIAM CARLOS WILLIAMS

A PAW ON THE SILL

ZEBRA

The eagle's shadow runs across the plain,
Towards the distant, nameless, air-blue mountains.
But the shadows of the round young Zebra
Sit close between their delicate hoofs all day,
    where they stand immovable,
And wait for the evening, wait to stretch out, blue,
Upon a plain, painted brick-red by the sunset,
And to wander to the water-hole.

ISAK DINESEN

CAT & THE WEATHER

Cat takes a look at the weather:
snow;
puts a paw on the sill;
his perch is piled, is a pillow.

Shape of his pad appears:
will it dig? No,
not like sand,
like his fur almost.

But licked, not liked:
too cold.
Insects are flying, fainting down.
He'll try

to bat one against the pane.
They have no body and no buzz,
and now his feet are wet;
it's a puzzle.

Shakes each leg,
then shakes his skin
to get the white flies off;
looks for his tail,

tells it to come on in
by the radiator.
World's turned queer
somehow: all white,

no smell. Well, here
inside it's still familiar.
He'll go to sleep until
it puts itself right.

MAY SWENSON

DOG AT NIGHT

At first he stirs uneasily in sleep
And since the moon does not run off, unfolds
Protesting paws. Grumbling that he must keep
Both eyes awake, he whimpers; then he scolds
And, rising to his feet, demands to know
The stranger's business. You who break the dark
With insolent light, who are you? Where do you go?
But nothing answers his indignant bark.
The moon ignores him, walking on as though
Dogs never were. Stiffened to fury now,
His small hairs stand upright, his howls come fast,
And terrible to hear the bow-wow
That tears the night. Stirred by this bugle-blast,
The farmer's bitch grows active; without pause
Summons her mastiff and the hound that lies
Three fields away to rally to the cause.
And the next county awakes. And miles beyond
Throats tear themselves and brassy lungs respond
With threats, entreaties, bellowings and cries,
Chasing the white intruder down the skies.

LOUIS UNTERMEYER

LANDSCAPE, DEER SEASON

Snorting his pleasure in the dying sun,
The buck surveys his commodious estate,
Not sighting the red nostrils of the gun
Until too late.

He is alone. His body holds stock-still,
Then like a monument it falls to earth;
While the blood-red target-sun, over our hill,
Topples to death.

BARBARA HOWES

TO CHRIST OUR LORD

The legs of the elk punctured the snow's crust
And wolves floated lightfooted on the land
Hunting Christmas elk living and frozen.
Indoors snow melted in a basin and a woman basted
A bird spread over coals by its wings and head.

Snow had sealed the windows; candles lit
The Christmas meal. The special grace chilled
The cooked bird, being long-winded and the room cold.
During the words a boy thought, is it fitting
To eat this creature killed on the wing?

For he had shot it himself, climbing out
Alone on snowshoes in the Christmas dawn,
The fallen snow swirling and the snowfall gone,
Heard its throat scream and the rifle shouted,
Watched it drop, and fished from the snow the dead.

He had not wanted to shoot. The sound
Of wings beating into the hushed morning
Had stirred his love, and the things
In his gloves froze, and he wondered
Even famishing, could he fire? Then he fired.

Now the grace praised his wicked act. At its end
The bird on the plate
Stared at his stricken appetite.
There had been nothing to do but surrender,
To kill and to eat; he ate as he had killed, with wonder.

At night on snowshoes on the drifting field
He wondered again, for whom had love stirred?
The stars glittered on the snow and nothing answered.
Then the swan spread her wings, cross of the cold north,
The pattern and mirror of the acts of earth.

GALWAY KINNELL

THE SHARK

My sweet, let me tell you about the Shark.
Though his eyes are bright, his thought is dark.
He's quiet—that speaks well of him.
So does the fact that he can swim.
But though he swims without a sound,
Wherever he swims he looks around
With those two bright eyes and that one dark thought.
He has only one but he thinks it a lot.
And the thought he thinks but can never complete
Is his long dark thought of something to eat.
Most anything does. And I have to add
That when he eats, his manners are bad.
He's a gulper, a ripper, a snatcher, a grabber.
Yes, his manners are drab. But his thought is drabber.
That one dark thought he can never complete
Of something—anything—somehow to eat.

Be careful where you swim, my sweet.

JOHN CIARDI

SHOPPING FOR MEAT IN WINTER

What lewd, naked, and revolting shape is this?
A frozen oxtail in the butcher's shop
Long and lifeless upon the huge block of wood
On which the ogre's axe begins *chop chop.*

The sun like incense fumes on the smoky glass,
The street frets with people, the winter wind
Throws knives, prices dangle from shoppers' mouths
While the grim vegetables, on parade, bring to mind

The great countryside bathed in golden sleep,
The trees, the bees, the soft peace everywhere—
I think of the cow's tail, how all summer long
It beat the shapes of harps into the air.

OSCAR WILLIAMS

THE SHARK'S PARLOR

The shark flopped on the porch, gating
    with salt-sand   driving back in
The nails he had pulled out   coughing
    chunks of his formless blood.
The screen door banged and tore off   he
    scrambled on his tail   slid
Curved   did a thing from another world
    and was out of his element and in
Our vacation paradise   cutting all four
    legs from under the dinner table
With one deep-water move   he unwove
    the rugs in a moment throwing pints
Of blood over everything we owned
    knocked the buck teeth out of my
    picture

His odd head full of crushed jelly-glass
    splinters and radio tubes thrashing
Among the pages of fan magazines   all
    the movie stars drenched in sea-blood.
Each time we thought he was dead   he
    struggled back and smashed
One more thing   in all coming back to
    die three or four more times
                after death.
At last we got him out   log-rolling him
    greasing his sandpaper skin
With lard to slide him   pulling on his
    chained lips as the tide came
Tumbled him down the steps as the first
    night wave went under the floor.

JAMES DICKEY

BEFORE DAWN

That practising bird is sharpening his call
on my sleep. I shall wring him feather from feather
and string up his pimpled skin, and grind his beak
for sweep dust. I shall debird him. Hold,
On what do I sharpen my cry?

ANN DARR

LOVE IS

a flock of birds, soaring, twisting, turning,
floating, lifting, swooping, landing, splitting into
pieces (individual birds) that can peck peck peck
before they once again unite in the flock that, rising,
goes reeling, shifting, flying (flying, that's the word
I was looking for) right out of sight.

ANN DARR

freddy the rat perishes

listen to me there have
been some doings here since last
i wrote there has been a battle
behind that rusty typewriter cover
in the corner
you remember freddy the rat well
freddy is no more but
he died game the other
day a stranger with a lot of
legs came into our
little circle a tough looking kid
he was with a bad eye

who are you said a thousand legs
if i bite you once
said the stranger you won t ask
again he he little poison tongue said
the thousand legs who gave you hydrophobia
i got it by biting myself said
the stranger i m bad keep away
from me where i step a weed dies
if i was to walk on your forehead it would
raise measles and if
you give me any lip i ll do it

they mixed it then
and the thousand legs succumbed
well we found out this fellow
was a tarantula he had come up from
south america in a bunch of bananas
for days he bossed us life

was not worth living he would stand in
the middle of the floor and taunt
us ha ha he would say where i
step a weed dies do
you want any of my game i was
raised on red pepper and blood i am
so hot if you scratch me i will light
like a match you better
dodge me when i m feeling mean and
i don t feel any other way i was nursed
on a tabasco bottle if i was to slap
your wrist in kindness you
would boil over like job and heaven
help you if i get angry give me
room i feel a wicked spell coming on

last night he made a break at freddy
the rat keep your distance
little one said freddy i m not
feeling well myself somebody poisoned some
cheese for me i m as full of
death as a drug store i
feel that i am going to die anyhow
come on little torpedo come on don t stop
to visit and search then they
went at it and both are no more ...

..............we dropped freddy
off the fire escape into the alley with
military honors

archy

DON MARQUIS

THESE NAKED IRON MUSCLES DRIPPING OIL

INVESTMENT

Vending myself,
A once machine,
I'm worth more dead,
With parts alive,
If my heart beats
For someone else,
My cornea sees
In another's eye.

Lungs, kidneys, blood,
My unscarred skin
Is above sex
Or next of kin;
They're hardly me,
Or so he says
Who chews my tongue,
Prays on my knees.

As noble thoughts
Caress all minds,
My lips may kiss
My cheeks when I'm
Scattered upon
A dozen forms
Or a club who share
Bits of my prime.

NORMAN NATHAN

MANHOLE COVERS

The beauty of manhole covers—what of that?
Like medals struck by a great savage khan,
Like Mayan calendar stones, unliftable, indecipherable,
Not like old electrum, chased and scored,
Mottoed and sculptured to a turn,
But notched and whelked and pocked and smashed
With the great company names:
Gentle Bethlehem, smiling United States.
This rustproof artifact of my street,
Long after roads are melted away, will lie
Sidewise in the graves of the iron-old world,
Bitten at the edges,
Strong with its cryptic American,
Its dated beauty.

KARL SHAPIRO

PORTRAIT OF A MACHINE

What nudity is beautiful as this
Obedient monster purring at its toil;
These naked iron muscles dripping oil;
And the sure-fingered rods that never miss.
This long and shiny flank of metal is
Magic that greasy labor cannot spoil;
While this vast engine that could rend the soil
Conceals its fury with a gentle hiss.

It does not vent its loathing, does not turn
Upon its makers with destroying hate.
It bears a deeper malice; throbs to earn
Its master's bread and lives to see this great
Lord of the earth, who rules but cannot learn,
Become the slave of what his slaves create.

LOUIS UNTERMEYER

THE PERFORATED SPIRIT

MORRIS BISHOP

The fellows up in Personnel,
  They have a set of cards on me.
The sprinkled perforations tell
  My individuality.

And what am I? I am a chart
  Upon the cards of I B M;
The secret places of the heart
  Have little secrecy for them.

It matters not how I may prate,
  They punch with punishments my scroll.
The files are masters of my fate,
  They are the captains of my soul.

Monday my brain began to buzz;
  I was in agony all night.
I found out what the trouble was:
  They had my paper clip too tight.

CENTRAL PARK TOURNEY

MILDRED WESTON

Cars
In the Park
With long spear lights
Ride at each other
Like armored knights;
Rush,
Miss the mark,
Pierce the dark,
Dash by!
Another two
Try.

Staged
In the Park
From dusk
To dawn,
The tourney goes on:
Rush,
Miss the mark,
Pierce the dark,
Dash by!
Another two
Try.

POEM TO BE READ AT 3 A.M.

Excepting the diner
on the outskirts
The town of Ladora
At 3 A.M.
Was dark but
For my headlights
And up in
One second-story room
A single light
Where someone
Was sick or
Perhaps reading
As I drove past
At seventy
Not thinking
This poem
Is for whoever
Had the light on

DONALD JUSTICE

WHAT DO I REALLY LOOK LIKE?

TRIOLET AGAINST SISTERS

Sisters are always drying their hair.
  Locked into rooms, alone,
They pose at the mirror, shoulders bare,
Trying this way and that their hair,
Or fly importunate down the stair
  To answer the phone.
Sisters are always drying their hair,
  Locked into rooms, alone.

PHYLLIS MCGINLEY

from "THE NIGHT BEFORE THE NIGHT BEFORE CHRISTMAS"

In her room that night she looks at herself in the mirror
And thinks: "Do I really look like *that?*"
She stares at her hair;
It's really a beautiful golden—anyway, yellow:
She brushes it with affection
And combs her bang back over so it slants.
How white her teeth are.
A turned-up nose . . .
No, it's no use.
She thinks: What do I *really* look like?
I don't know.

Not really.
Really.

RANDALL JARRELL

PROLETARIAN PORTRAIT

A big young bareheaded woman
in an apron

Her hair slicked back standing
on the street

One stockinged foot toeing
the sidewalk

Her shoe in her hand. Looking
intently into it

She pulls out the paper insole
to find the nail

That has been hurting her.

WILLIAM CARLOS WILLIAMS

O CATCH MISS DAISY PINKS

O catch Miss Daisy Pinks
Undressing behind her hair;
She slides open like a drawer
Oiled miraculously by a stare.

O the long cool limbs,
The ecstatic shot of hair,
And untroubled eyes
With their thousand-mile stare.

Her eyes are round as marigolds;
Her navel drips with honey;
Her pulse is even, and her laugh
Crackles like paper money.

ALISTAIR CAMPBELL

WHAT WAS *HER NAME?*

Someone must make out the cards
for the funeral of the filing clerk.
Poor bony rack with her buzzard's
jowled eyes bare as a dirk
and as sharp for dead fact, she
could have done it better than anyone
will do it for her. It will be,
to be sure, done.
And the flowers sent. And the office closed
for the half day it takes
for whatever we are supposed
to make of the difference it makes
to file the filing clerk
where we can forget her.

Someone will do the work
she used to do better.

JOHN CIARDI

COCAINE LIL

Did you ever hear about Cocaine Lil?
She lived in Cocaine town on Cocaine hill,
She had a cocaine dog and a cocaine cat,
They fought all night with the cocaine rat.

She had cocaine hair on her cocaine head.
She wore a snow-bird hat and sleigh-riding clothes.
She had a cocaine dress that was poppy red.
On her coat she wore a crimson, cocaine rose.

Big gold chariots on the Milky Way,
Snakes and elephants silver and gray,
O the cocaine blues they make me sad,
O the cocaine blues make me feel bad.

Lil went to a "snow" party one cold night,
And the way she "sniffed" was sure a fright.
There was Hophead Mag with Dopey Slim,
Kankakee Liz with Yen Shee Jim.

There was Hasheesh Nell and the Poppy Face Kid,
Climbed up snow ladders and down they slid;
There was Stepladder Kit, he stood six feet,
And the Sleigh-riding Sisters that are hard to beat.

Along in the morning about half-past three
They were all lit up like a Christmas tree;
Lil got home and started to go to bed,
Took another "sniff" and it knocked her dead.

They laid her out in her cocaine clothes.
She wore a snow-bird hat and a crimson rose;
On her headstone you'll find this refrain:
"She died as she lived, sniffing cocaine."

ANONYMOUS

THE YOUNG GIRL'S SONG

I have just now
Become a woman,
Just now have I
Begun to feel
The urgings
Of my new womanhood.
I am not beautiful.
The glass does
Not lie to me.
I know I am plain,
Plain as my mother,
And she
Has told me,
"Take up your broom,
Sweep clean.
Learn well
The simple ways of women,
And you will
Become beautiful
In the eyes
Of your lover.
So it was
With your father,
So it was
With me."
I have learned well
The simple ways of women.
Each morning
I open the doors
Of my house
And sweep
To the middle
Of our stone street.
It was so
That I met
My lover.
He, hammer and saw
In hand
Half trotting
To his daily work,

Helping to build our town.
It was so,
As the morning
Passed, that we began.
First only with
"Buenos días,"
Then more and more
Until tonight
In the full light
Of the moon
He will bring music
To my window.
And, as is the custom,
I shall pretend
Not to hear it,
Pretend that my
Heart is not leaping,
That my arms
And my thighs
Are not aching
For his presence.
And as the
Fingers of the moonlight
Feel their way
Through the iron bars
That protect the windows
Of my humble house,
He will behold
A clean, clean—
Swept floor,
And know that
He is wooing
One well versed
In the simple ways
Of the woman.
Blessed am I
For being
As beautifully homely as I am,
And for feeling
And loving deeply.

ALVIN J. GORDON

LET ME CELEBRATE YOU

A DIALOGUE OF WATCHING

Let me celebrate you. I
Have never known anyone
More beautiful than you. I
Walking beside you, watching
You move beside me, watching
That still grace of hand and thigh,
Watching your face change with words
You do not say, watching your
Solemn eyes as they turn to me,
Or turn inward, full of knowing,
Slow or quick, watching your full
Lips part and smile or turn grave,
Watching your narrow waist, your
Proud buttocks in their grace, like
A sailing swan, an animal,
Free, your own, and never
To be subjugated, but
Abandoned, as I am to you,
Overhearing your perfect
Speech of motion, of love and
Trust and security as
You feed or play with our children.
I have never known any
One more beautiful than you.

KENNETH REXROTH

FIRST PERSON DEMONSTRATIVE

I'd rather
heave half a brick than say
I love you, though I do
I'd rather
crawl in a hole than call you
darling, though you are
I'd rather
wrench off an arm than hug you
    though
it's what I long to do
I'd rather
gather a posy of poison ivy than
ask if you love me

so if my

hair doesn't stand on end it's
    because
it knows its place
and if I
don't take a bite of your ear
    it's because
I never tease it
and if my
heart isn't in my mouth it's
    because
gristle gripes my guts
and if you
miss the message better get new
glasses and read it twice

PHYLLIS GOTLIEB

WHERE HAVE YOU GONE?

where have you gone . . .

with your confident
walk . . . with
your crooked smile . . .

why did you leave
me
when you took your
laughter
and departed
Are you aware that
with you
went the sun
all light
and what few stars
there were . . . ?

where have you gone
with your confident
walk your
crooked smile the
rent money
in one pocket and
my heart
in
another. . . .

MARI EVANS

GIRL, BOY, FLOWER, BICYCLE

This girl
Waits at the corner for
This boy
Freewheeling on his bicycle.
She holds
A flower in her hand
A gold flower
In her hands she holds
The sun.
With power between his thighs
The boy
Comes smiling to her
He rides
A bicycle that glitters like
The wind.
This boy this girl
They walk
In step with the wind
Arm in arm
They climb the level street
To where
Laid on the glittering handlebars
The flower
Is round and shining as
The sun.

M. K. JOSEPH

WHEN I WAS ONE-AND-TWENTY

When I was one-and-twenty
  I heard a wise man say,
"Give crowns and pounds and guineas
  But not your heart away;
Give pearls away and rubies
  But keep your fancy free."
But I was one-and-twenty,
  No use to talk to me.

When I was one-and-twenty
  I heard him say again,
"The heart out of the bosom
  Was never given in vain;
'Tis paid with sighs a plenty
  And sold for endless rue."
And I am two-and-twenty,
  And oh, 'tis true, 'tis true.

A. E. HOUSMAN

OH, WHEN I WAS IN LOVE WITH YOU

Oh, when I was in love with you,
  Then I was clean and brave,
And miles around the wonder grew
  How well did I behave.

And now the fancy passes by,
  And nothing will remain,
And miles around they'll say that I
  Am quite myself again.

A. E. HOUSMAN

THE MARITAL JOURNEY

Little Lemlem was married, at last!
She was fifteen.
Now the village people cannot say:
"She remained standing,"
For that is what they say of girls
For whom the fortune of marriage does not come
at comfortable times.

Little Lemlem went away,
She followed the narrow path,
The winding path,
Over the mountains,
Where it is breezy and cool,
She followed the steps of her husband.

Her man built a "gojo" for her
in that far-away land,
He built it on a mountain side
Where she could see the water spring below
And the village women with their water jars
Carrying water home.

She perceived her world:
There was a church on a hill top,
St. Mary's Church it was,
And beyond was a waving barley land.

On the mountain sides
Were more dwellings of tillers of the land
Raisers of barley, and their clans.
It was a land of quiet people
Busy at heart.

"So this be my home," she said,
"My land.
"May it be blessed;
"May it have peace for me,
"For home is there where the heart is at rest."

This she said in faith
For she was taught to have faith in the land.
And with hope,
And with a dream,
She set herself to a task—
An old ancestral task—
Of raising a new generation of tillers of the land,
Raisers of barley,
Quiet people,
Busy at heart.

HAILU ARAAYA

INDEX OF AUTHORS AND TITLES

INDEX OF FIRST LINES

ACKNOWLEDGMENTS

"Plan," by Rod McKuen: copyright © 1968 by Rod McKuen. Reprinted from *Lonesome Cities,* by Rod McKuen, by permission of Random House, Inc.

"Reel One," by Adrien Stoutenburg: reprinted with the permission of Charles Scribner's Sons from *Heroes, Advise Us,* by Adrien Stoutenburg. Copyright © 1964 by Adrien Stoutenburg.

"Ball Game," by Richard Eberhart: copyright © 1967 by Richard Eberhart. First appeared in *New American Review #1.* Reprinted with permission of the author.

"Horror Movie," by Howard Moss: from *Swimmer in the Air.* Copyright © 1957 by Howard Moss. Reprinted with permission of the author.

"The High School Band," by Reed Whittemore: reprinted with permission of The Macmillan Company from *The Self-Made Man,* by Reed Whittemore. © by Reed Whittemore, 1959.

"The World Is a Beautiful Place," by Lawrence Ferlinghetti: from *A Coney Island of the Mind.* Copyright 1955 by Lawrence Ferlinghetti. Reprinted by permission of New Directions Publishing Corporation.

"To My Brother Miguel: *in memoriam,*" by Cesar Vallejo: reprinted from *Neruda and Vallejo: Selected Poems,* edited by Robert Bly, Beacon Press, 1971. Copyright © 1962 by The Sixties Press. Reprinted by permission of The Sixties Press.

"The Whipping," by Robert Hayden: from *Selected Poems.* Copyright © 1966 by Robert Hayden. Reprinted by permission of October House, Inc.

"At 79th and Park," by Barbara Howes: copyright © 1967 by Barbara Howes. Reprinted by permission of the author. First appeared in *New American Review #2.*

"When Mahalia Sings," by Quandra Prettyman: from *I Am the Darker Brother.* Copyright © 1968 by Quandra Prettyman Stadler. Used by permission of the author.

"American Rhapsody (4)," by Kenneth Fearing: used by permission of the Executors of the Estate of Kenneth Fearing. Copr. © 1940, 1968 by Kenneth Fearing. First appeared in *The New Yorker.*

"Modifications," by Ronald Koertge: from *Some Haystacks Don't Even Have Any Needles.* Reprinted by arrangement with the author

"He Don't know the *Inside* Feel," by Herbert R. Adams: Copyright © 1967, *English Journal.* Reprinted with the permission of the National Council of Teachers of English and Herbert R. Adams.

"teechur," by Dick Higgins: from *foew&ombwhnw.* Copyright © 1969 by Something Else Press. All rights reserved. Used by permission of the publisher and the author.

"Freedom," by William Stafford: copyright © 1969 by William Stafford. First appeared in *New American Review #2*. Reprinted by permission of the author.

"Transcontinent," by Donald Hall: reprinted by permission of Curtis Brown Ltd. and Saturday Review, Inc. Copyright © 1959 by Saturday Review, Inc.

"Wires," by Philip Larkin: reprinted from *The Less Deceived,* © copyright by The Marvell Press 1955, 1971, by permission of The Marvell Press, Hessle, Yorkshire, England.

"Buffalo Dusk," by Carl Sandburg: from *Smoke and Steel,* by Carl Sandburg. Copyright 1920 by Harcourt Brace Jovanovich, Inc., renewed 1948 by Carl Sandburg. Reprinted by permission of the publisher.

"Cowboy Song," by Charles Causley: from *Union Street,* by Charles Causley (Rupert Hart-Davis Ltd.). Reprinted by permission of the author and David Higham Associates.

"Staying Alive," by David Wagoner: from *Staying Alive,* by David Wagoner. Copyright © 1966 by Indiana University Press. Reprinted by permission of the publisher.

"The Motorcyclist's Song" by DeWitt Bell: copyright © 1963 by The Atlantic Monthly Company, Boston, Mass. Reprinted by permission.

"Upstream," by Carl Sandburg: from *Slabs of the Sunburnt West,* by Carl Sandburg. Copyright 1922 by Harcourt Brace Jovanovich, Inc., renewed 1950 by Carl Sandburg. Reprinted by permission of the publishers.

"Hunger," by Lennart Bruce: reprinted by permission of Lennart Bruce and *Saturday Review*. Copyright © 1969 Saturday Review, Inc.

"Thief Jones," by Robert P. Tristram Coffin: reprinted with permission of The Macmillan Company from *Collected Poems* by Robert P. Tristram Coffin. Copyright 1937 by The Macmillan Company, renewed 1965 by Margaret Coffin Halvosa.

"Mr. Flood's Party," by Edwin Arlington Robinson: reprinted with permission of The Macmillan Company from *Collected Poems* by Edwin Arlington Robinson. Copyright 1921 by Edwin Arlington Robinson, renewed 1949 by Ruth Nivison.

"The Old Men Admiring Themselves in the Water," by William Butler Yeats: reprinted with permission of the author, Macmillan & Co. Ltd., and The Macmillan Company from *Collected Poems* by William Butler Yeats. Copyright 1903 by The Macmillan Company, renewed 1931 by William Butler Yeats. Used by permission of The Macmillan Company, Michael B. Yeats and Macmillan & Co. Ltd.

"To an Athlete Dying Young," by A. E. Housman: from "A Shropshire Lad," Authorised Edition, from *The Collected Poems of A. E. Housman*. Copyright 1939, 1940, © 1967, 1968 by Robert E. Symons. Reprinted by permission of Holt, Rinehart and Winston, Inc., and The Society of Authors as the literary representative of the Estate of A. E. Housman, and Jonathan Cape Ltd., publishers of A. E. Housman's *Collected Poems*.

"Ex-Basketball Player," by John Updike: from *The Carpentered Hen and Other Tame Creatures,* by John Updike. Copyright © 1957 by John Updike. Reprinted by permission of Harper & Row Publishers, Inc.

"Richard Cory," by Edwin Arlington Robinson: reprinted by permission of Charles Scribner's Sons from *The Children of the Night,* by Edwin Arlington Robinson (1897).

"On Hurricane Jackson," by Alan Dugan: copyright © 1961 by Alan Dugan. From *Poems,* Yale University Press. Used by permission of the author.

"The Loser," by Charles Bukowski: copyright © 1960. First appeared in *The Sparrow Magazine.* Used by permission of *The Sparrow Magazine.*

"The Vanity of Human Wishes," by John Leax: from *The English Record* (Vol. 20, No. 2). By permission of New York State English Council and the author.

"Cowboys: One, Two, Three," by Rod McKuen: copyright © 1967, 1968 by Editions Chanson Co. Reprinted from *Lonesome Cities,* by Rod McKuen, by permission of Random House, Inc.

"Epitaph on a Tyrant," by W. H. Auden: copyright 1940 and renewed 1968 by W. H. Auden. Reprinted from *Collected Shorter Poems 1927–1957* by W. H. Auden, by permission of Random House, Inc., and Faber and Faber Ltd.

"Bowery," by David Ignatow: copyright © 1948 by David Ignatow. Reprinted from *Poems 1934–1969* by David Ignatow, by permission of Wesleyan University Press.

"The Creation," by James Weldon Johnson: from *God's Trombones,* by James Weldon Johnson. Copyright 1927 by The Viking Press, Inc. Renewed 1955 by Grace Nail Johnson. Reprinted by permission of The Viking Press, Inc.

"Fueled," by Marcie Hans: from *Serve Me a Slice of Moon,* © 1965 by Marcie Hans. Reprinted by permission of Harcourt Brace Jovanovich, Inc.

"The Stump," by Donald Hall: from *The Alligator Bride: Poems New and Selected,* by Donald Hall. Copyright © 1964 by Donald Hall. Reprinted by permission of Harper & Row, Publishers, Inc.

"Fable for When There's No Way Out," by May Swenson: reprinted with the permission of Charles Scribner's Sons from *Half Sun Half Sleep,* by May Swenson. Copyright © 1967 by May Swenson.

"Earth," by Oliver Herford: reprinted with the permission of Charles Scribner's Sons from *The Bashful Earthquake,* by Oliver Herford (1898).

"Summer Holiday," by Robinson Jeffers: copyright 1925 and renewed 1953 by Robinson Jeffers. Reprinted from *The Selected Poetry of Robinson Jeffers,* by permission of Random House, Inc.

"Dream Variation," by Langston Hughes: copyright 1926 by Alfred A. Knopf, Inc., and renewed 1954 by Langston Hughes. Reprinted from *Selected Poems* by Langston Hughes, by permission of the publisher.

"The Death of the Sports-Car Driver," by Jonathan Aaron: from *The Yale Review* (Vol. 59, No. 3). Copyright © 1970 by Yale University. Used by permission of *The Yale Review.*

"Between the World and Me," by Richard Wright: copyright © 1935 by *The Partisan Review.* Reprinted by permission of Paul R. Reynolds, Inc., 599 Fifth Avenue, New York, N.Y. 10017.

"Malfunction," by Richard E. Albert: copyright © 1966 by Harper's Magazine, Inc. Reprinted from the February 1966 issue of *Harper's Magazine* by permission of the author.

"Fire and Ice," by Robert Frost: from *The Poetry of Robert Frost,* edited by Edward Connery Lathem. Copyright 1916, 1923, © 1969 by Holt, Rinehart and Winston, Inc. Copyright 1944, 1951 by Robert Frost. Reprinted by permission of Holt, Rinehart and Winston, Inc.

"The Quarry," by W. H. Auden: copyright 1937 and renewed 1965 by W. H. Auden. Reprinted from *Collected Shorter Poems 1927–1957* by W. H. Auden, by permission of Random House, Inc., and Faber and Faber Ltd.

"Out, Out—" by Robert Frost: from *The Poetry of Robert Frost,* edited by Edward

Connery Lathem. Copyright 1916, 1923, © 1969 by Holt, Rinehart and Winston, Inc. Copyright 1944, 1951 by Robert Frost. Reprinted by permission of Holt, Rinehart and Winston, Inc.

"Tract," by William Carlos Williams: from *The Collected Earlier Poems,* copyright 1938 by William Carlos Williams. Reprinted by permission of New Directions Publishing Corporation.

"Zebra," by Isak Dinesen: from *Out of Africa,* by Isak Dinesen. Copyright 1937 and renewed 1965 by Rungstedlundfonden. Reprinted by permission of Random House, Inc., and Putnam & Co. Ltd., the British publisher of *Out of Africa.*

"Cat & the Weather," by May Swenson: reprinted with the permission of Charles Scribner's Sons from *To Mix With Time,* by May Swenson. Copyright © 1963 by May Swenson.

"Dog at Night," by Louis Untermeyer: copyright 1928 by Harcourt Brace Jovanovich, Inc., renewed 1956 by Louis Untermeyer. Reprinted from *Long Feud,* by Louis Untermeyer, by permission of the publisher.

"Landscape, Deer Season," by Barbara Howes: copyright © 1962 by Barbara Howes. Reprinted from *Looking Up at Leaves,* by Barbara Howes, by permission of Alfred A. Knopf, Inc.

"To Christ Our Lord," by Galway Kinnell: from *What a Kingdom It Was,* by Galway Kinnell. Copyright © 1960 by Galway Kinnell. Reprinted by permission of the publisher, Houghton Mifflin Company.

"The Shark," by John Ciardi: copyright © 1967 by Saturday Review, Inc. First appeared in *Saturday Review.* Used by permission.

"Shopping for Meat in Winter," by Oscar Williams: from *Selected Poems,* copyright 1947, by permission of the Executors of the Estate of Oscar Williams.

"The Shark's Parlor," by James Dickey: Copyright © 1965 by James Dickey. Reprinted from *Buckdancer's Choice,* by James Dickey, by permission of Wesleyan University Press. This poem first appeared in *The New Yorker.*

"Before Dawn," by Ann Darr: reprinted by permission of *The New Republic.* © 1970, Harrison-Blaine of New Jersey, Inc.

"Love Is," by Ann Darr: reprinted by permission of *The New Republic.* © 1970, Harrison-Blaine of New Jersey, Inc.

"Freddy the rat perishes," by Don Marquis: from the book *Archy and Mehitabel,* by Don Marquis. Copyright 1927 by Doubleday & Company, Inc. Reprinted by permission of Doubleday & Company, Inc.

"Investment," by Norman Nathan: copyright © 1970 by Saturday Review, Inc. From Martin Levin's "Phoenix Nest," *Saturday Review.* Used by permission of *Saturday Review* and Martin Levin.

"Manhole Covers," by Karl Shapiro: copyright © 1962 by Karl Shapiro. Reprinted from *Selected Poems* by Karl Shapiro, by permission of Random House, Inc. Originally appeared in *The New Yorker.*

"Portrait of a Machine," by Louis Untermeyer: copyright 1923 by Harcourt Brace Jovanovich, Inc., copyright 1951 by Louis Untermeyer. Reprinted from *Long Feud,* by Louis Untermeyer, by permission of the publisher.

"The Perforated Spirit," by Morris Bishop: copr. © 1955 The New Yorker Magazine, Inc. Reprinted by permission.

"Central Park Tourney," by Mildred Weston: copr. © 1953 The New Yorker Magazine, Inc. Reprinted by permission.

"Poem To Be Read at 3 A.M.," by Donald Justice: copyright © 1967 by Donald Justice. A section of "American Sketches" in *Night Light,* by Donald Justice. Reprinted by permission of Wesleyan University Press.

"Triolet Against Sisters," by Phyllis McGinley: from *Times Three,* by Phyllis McGinley. Copyright © 1959 by Phyllis McGinley. Originally appeared in *The New Yorker.* Reprinted by permission of The Viking Press, Inc.

From "The Night Before the Night Before Christmas" by Randall Jarrell: Reprinted with the permission of Farrar, Straus & Giroux, Inc., from *The Complete Poems* by Randall Jarrell, Copyright © 1949, 1969, by Mrs. Randall Jarrell.

"Proletarian Portrait," by William Carlos Williams: from *The Collected Earlier Poems.* Copyright 1938 by William Carlos Williams. Reprinted by permission of New Directions Publishing Corporation.

"O Catch Miss Daisy Pinks," by Alistair Campbell: from *Mine Eyes Dazzle,* published by Pegasus Press, Christchurch, New Zealand. Used by permission.

"What *Was* Her Name?" by John Ciardi: from *Person to Person,* by John Ciardi. Copyright 1964 by Rutgers, The State University. Reprinted by permission of the author.

"The Young Girl's Song," by Alvin J. Gordon: from *Brooms of Mexico,* published by Best-West Publications, Box 757, Palm Desert, California. Used by permission of the author.

"A Dialogue of Watching," by Kenneth Rexroth: from *The Collected Shorter Poems.* Copyright © 1956 by New Directions Publishing Corporation. Reprinted by permission of New Directions Publishing Corporation.

"First Person Demonstrative," by Phyllis Gotlieb: from *Ordinary Moving,* by Phyllis Gotlieb. Reprinted by permission of The Oxford University Press, Canadian Branch.

"Where Have You Gone?" by Mari Evans: from *New Negro Poets: USA,* edited by Langston Hughes. Reprinted by permission of the author.

"Girl, Boy, Flower, Bicycle," by M. K. Joseph: from *Voices: The Second Book,* edited by Geoffrey Summerfield. Reprinted by permission of the publisher, Penguin Books Ltd.

"When I Was One-and-Twenty," by A. E. Housman: from "A Shropshire Lad," Authorised Edition, from *The Collected Poems of A. E. Housman.* Copyright 1939, 1940, © 1959 by Holt, Rinehart and Winston, Inc. Copyright © 1967, 1968 by Robert E. Symons. Reprinted by permission of Holt, Rinehart and Winston, Inc., and The Society of Authors as the literary representative of the Estate of A. E. Housman, and Jonathan Cape Ltd., publishers of A. E. Housman's *Collected Poems.*

"Oh, When I Was in Love with You," by A. E. Housman: from "A Shropshire Lad," Authorised Edition, from *The Collected Poems of A. E. Housman.* Copyright 1939, 1940, © 1959 by Holt, Rinehart and Winston, Inc. Copyright © 1967, 1968 by Robert E. Symons. Reprinted by permission of Holt, Rinehart and Winston, Inc., and The Society of Authors as the literary representative of the Estate of A. E. Housman, and Jonathan Cape Ltd., publishers of A. E. Housman's *Collected Poems.*

"The Marital Journey," by Hailu Araaya: from "Poems from Ethiopia" collected by Hailu Araaya, published in *Teachers College Record* (Vol. 71, No. 1, September 1969). Used by permission of *Teachers College Record* and the author.

ABOUT THE EDITOR

Richard Peck was born in Decatur, Illinois. He studied at Exeter University in England and graduated from DePauw University. He is the co-editor of an essay collection, *Edge of Awareness,* and the editor of one previous collection of contemporary poetry, *Sounds and Silences.* His own poetry has appeared in *Saturday Review.*

Mr. Peck is currently on leave from teaching duties at Hunter College and at Hunter College High School, New York City. He has recently served as assistant director of The Council for Basic Education, Washington, D.C.

THIS BOOK WAS SET IN

HELVETICA, FUTURA, AND BASKERVILLE TYPES BY

BROWN BROS. LINOTYPERS, INC.

IT WAS PRINTED BY

HALLIDAY LITHOGRAPH CORPORATION

AND BOUND BY

MONTAUK BOOK MFG. CO., INC.

DESIGNED BY LARRY KAMP